A Turkish Rosh Hashanah

Etan Basseri

ILLUSTRATED BY
Zeynep Özatalay

Kalaniot Books
Moosic, Pennsylvania

The sun shimmered off the fishing boats as the fog cleared over Istanbul's harbor. "Nona!" called Rafael, running to greet his grandmother, who was walking with his cousins Alegra and León.

"Rafaeliko! *Buenos dias, mi alma!* Thank you for helping us with our Rosh Hashanah shopping."

"Is tonight when we get to make New Year's wishes on those special foods, Nona?" asked Rafael.

"Yes. It wouldn't be a Rosh Hashanah dinner without the *yehi ratzones*!"

"Delicious wishes for an *Anyada buena*, a happy New Year!" agreed Alegra.

At the crowded market, Nona checked her list. "You kids will need to get pomegranates, leeks, and a whole fish—head and all. I'm off to get the apples, beets, pumpkin, and dates. Now stick together, *ijos*," advised Nona, giving Rafael some coins. "And make sure you buy pomegranates only from Senyor Benezra. We'll meet back here."

The cousin's first stop was the fisherman's stall. Alegra selected the freshest fish she could find and a snack of fried fish for herself and her cousins.

Suddenly she froze. It was a cat. Very little scared Rafael's feisty cousin, but cats were different. They just seemed so creepy!

"He's just after your fish. Cats love *pishkado*! Come here, kitty," said Rafael, offering the cat a piece of his fried fish snack.

At the next stall Rafael turned to his shy cousin, León. "Are you feeling brave?" León nodded.

"Can I help you?" asked the smiling shopkeeper.

León just stood there, nervous and silent as the line got longer and longer. Rafael put a reassuring hand on his shoulder, and Alegra gave her cousin a warm smile. Finally, León took a deep breath and whispered, *"Prassa*, please."

"Ah, leeks!" said the shopkeeper.

"Good job, León!" said Rafael as he paid.

Just then Alegra tugged on Rafael's sleeve. "That cat is back, and it's brought a friend!" The cats stared at Alegra and flicked their tails. Definitely creepy.

Rafael stepped between her and the cats as León handed them another piece of fried fish. "Here, kitties." Rafael beckoned his cousins. "Let's go!"

The cousins' final stop was Senyor Benezra's stall. "Can't we just get pomegranates somewhere else?" complained Rafael when he saw the long line.

"Nona told us we had to shop at Senyor Benezra's! He has the best pomegranates in Istanbul," Alegra replied, leaning closer and whispering, "I've heard that his pomegranates are so sweet because he sings to them."

כפלח הרמון רקתך מבעד לצמתך

Finally, it was their turn. Rafael marveled at the bright red fruits. "Senyor Benezra, is it true that you sing to your *agranadas*?" he asked.

"Why yes!" he answered. And picking up a fruit with a perfect crown, Senyor Benezra sang to his pomegranate queen: "Your face behind your veil gleams like a pomegranate," blowing her a sweet kiss. They all laughed—except Alegra, who was staring at not just one cat, not two cats, but five cats. "Rafael!" she cried.

"Let's make a run for it," he said, handing over some coins and placing three bright red pomegranates in his basket. "Thank you, Senyor Benezra!"

The cousins were quickly making their way through the market and back to Nona when all of a sudden, a big boy stepped out and blocked their path. "What's this?" the boy asked, pulling out a pomegranate from Rafael's basket and shoving him.

"Oh! It's a ball!" He threw it against the stone wall. The pomegranate exploded. Red juice and seeds flew everywhere.

Alegra stood up straight. Her heart was pounding, but she looked right into the boy's eyes. "Leave us alone!" While creepy cats might frighten Alegra, she wasn't afraid of some bully—especially one that was threatening her cousins.

"Yah! Leave us alone," yelled little León. Both Rafael and Alegra turned toward their cousin in surprise. They had never heard León speak this loudly.

"Are you gonna stop me, tiny one?" the bully teased. "You . . . ah . . . ah . . . ah . . . choo! Shoo, cats! Ugh! They always make me sneeze . . . ah . . . ah . . . choo!"

The cats rushed towards the boy and—bang!—he bumped into a board that fell onto a box that tipped a barrel and—splat! The bully was completely covered in stinky fish scraps. And as the cats swarmed the boy to get to their fishy treat, the cousins gave each other a satisfied nod and walked off to meet Nona.

Later that afternoon, the entire family gathered at Nona's house. "*Anyada buena*, a very happy New Year, everyone," welcomed Nona. "Thank you to León, Alegra, and Rafael. You helped each other today, and because of your teamwork we can enjoy these delicious *yehi ratzones*. Each is a symbol of good wishes for the new year."

"We have apples for sweetness, beets for freedom, dates for peace, pumpkin for forgiveness," said Nona.

"What else am I missing, León?" asked Nona.

"*Prassa!*" he cried.

"Yes, leeks for friends who protect us," Nona replied.

"Rafael, what have I forgotten?" asked Nona.

"There's pomegranates so that our good deeds will be as many as the seeds inside," said Rafael.

"What else, Alegra?" Nona asked.
"A fish head!" announced Alegra. *"Kavesa de pishkado* so that this year we will be leaders at the top."

"And not behind, like the tail," Nona chimed in. "Especially a cat's tail!" Alegra said. Everyone laughed. It was going to be a great year!

History of Jewish Life in Turkey

Jews have a long history in Turkey, dating back over two thousand years. Sephardic Jews expelled from Spain in 1492 found refuge in the Ottoman Empire, whose capital was the city of Istanbul, known at that time as Constantinople. Under Ottoman rule, Jews of many backgrounds thrived and maintained distinct communities often based on their country or city of origin. Ladino, also known as Judeo-Spanish, was the spoken and written language of the Sephardic community. Starting in the late nineteenth century, the Ottoman Empire began to decline, and life became more difficult for the Jewish community. Seeking greater safety, freedom, and economic opportunities, many emigrated to the United States, Latin America, and Israel. Today only a few small Jewish communities remain in Turkey.

Celebrating Rosh Hashanah

Rosh Hashanah is the Jewish New Year, a time dedicated to reflecting on the previous year, praying for a good year to come, and celebrating with family and friends. We mark the holiday by sounding the shofar (ram's horn) and special festive meals that often include apples, honey, and round challah.

You may be familiar with a Passover seder, the ritual meal commemorating the Israelites' escape from Egypt. But did you know that many Sephardic, Mizrachi, and Hasidic Jews also do another seder during the Rosh Hashanah holiday? Much like the special foods included in the Passover seder, the Rosh Hashanah seder (*yehi ratzones* in Ladino) incorporates symbolic foods to express hopes for a prosperous new year. The cooked head of a fish or sheep, chosen based on local availability, symbolizes the desire for the self-determination of the Jewish people, aspiring to be "like the head and not like the tail." A pomegranate is used to convey the prayer that the merits of the Jewish people in the upcoming year will be as abundant as the seeds of the fruit. Some symbols involve phonetic wordplay, such as leeks (*karti* in Aramaic), representing the wish for the enemies of the Jewish people to be "cut off" (*karet* in Hebrew). These prayers reflect the challenging times faced by the Jewish community throughout history and the strength we draw from this annual tradition.

Senyor Benezra's Song

In the story Senyor Benezra sings to his pomegranates: "Your face behind your veil gleams like a pomegranate."

כפלח הרמון רקתך מבעד לצמתך

This is a line from the Song of Solomon in the Bible (Song of Songs 6:7). This beautiful poem is often seen as a metaphor for the loving relationship between God and the people of Israel, with God portrayed as the groom and Israel as the bride. We read this line during the *yehi ratzones* when we eat the pomegranate.

Ladino Glossary

agranada: Pomegranate.
Anyada buena: Happy New Year.
buenas dias: Good morning.
ijos: Kids.
kavesa de pishkado: Fish head.
mi alma: My dear.
nona: Grandma.
pishkado: Fish.
prassa: Leek.
senyor: Mister.
yehi ratzones: A Jewish ritual service of symbolic foods and prayers observed on the eve of the New Year.

For Sonya
—E. B.

*For Istanbul, my beloved city,
and all the children who have run on its pavements for centuries.*
—Z. Ö.

AUTHOR'S ACKNOWLEDGMENTS

I would like to thank my family and friends for teaching me the traditions of the Seattle Sephardic community, whose roots are in Turkey and Rhodes, especially my mother-in-law, Janet (Benezra) Jassen. I'm also grateful to Paul Ichilcik, Rachel Amado-Bortnick, and Ty Alhadeff for their expertise and advice and to Congregation Sephardic Bikur Holim for the use of their library.

*All Kalaniot Books have accompanying activity guides.
Download them for free at KalaniotBooks.com.*

Text copyright © 2024 by Etan Basseri
Illustrations copyright © 2024 by Zeynep Özatalay
Published by Kalaniot Books, an imprint of Endless Mountains Publishing Company
72 Glenmaura National Boulevard, Suite 104B, Moosic, Pennsylvania 18507
www.KalaniotBooks.com
All rights reserved. No part of this book may be reproduced, stored in a retrieval system, or transmitted in any form or by any means—electronic, mechanical, photocopying, recording, or otherwise—without the prior written permission of Endless Mountains Publishing Company, except for the inclusion of brief quotations in an acknowledged review.
Library of Congress Control Number: 2024930253
ISBN: 978-1-962011-97-6
Printed in China
First Printing